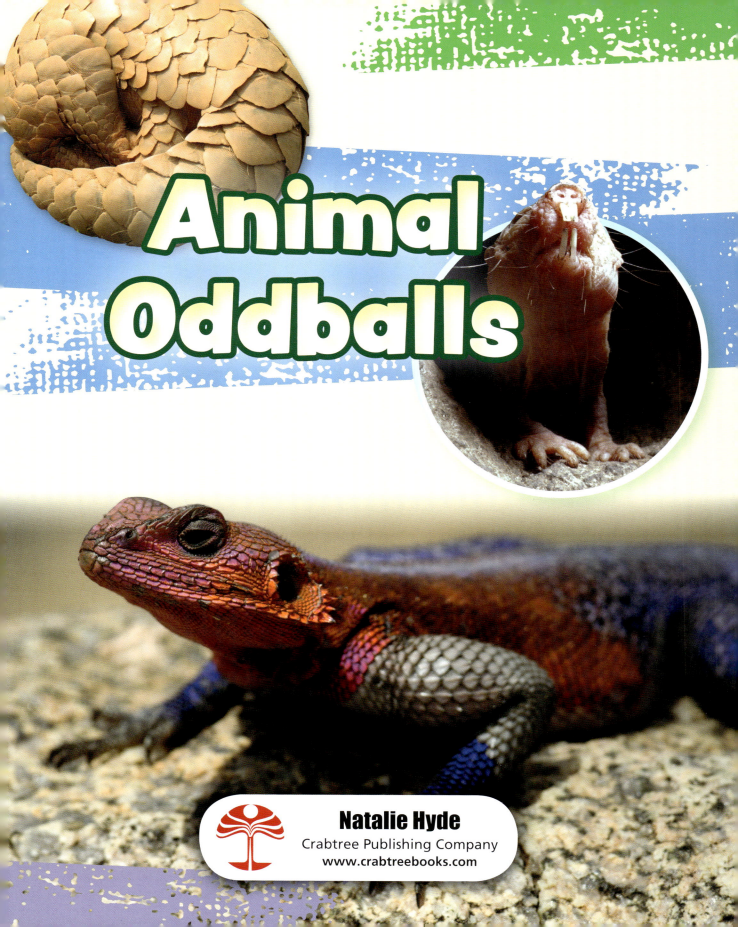
Animal Oddballs

Natalie Hyde
Crabtree Publishing Company
www.crabtreebooks.com

CRABTREE
PUBLISHING COMPANY
WWW.CRABTREEBOOKS.COM

Author:
Natalie Hyde
Editorial director:
Kathy Middleton
Editor:
Sonya Newland
Proofreaders:
Izzi Howell, Crystal Sikkens
Graphic design:
Richard Parker
Image research:
Natalie Hyde and Sonya Newland
Production coordinator and prepress:
Tammy McGarr
Print coordinator:
Katherine Berti

Images:
Alamy: 11b (blickwinkel), 13b (royalty free Arctos photos), 19b (Sanamyan), 23b (DPA Picture Alliance), 26–27 all (Natural History Library), 28 (Minden Pictures), 29b (Steve Bloom Images); Getty Images: 17b (Mark Newman); Shutterstock: 4 (Agnieszka Bacal), 5 (S.Rohrlach), 6 (John Carnemolla), 7tl (Eric Isselee), 7tr (worldswildlifewonders), 7b (Nicolas Primola), 8 (Luca Nichetti), 9t (Mogens Trolle), 9b (bayazed), 10–11 (Lapis2380), 11t (Arm001), 12 (Positive Snapshot), 13t (Eugene Troskie), 14 (G.J. Verspui), 15t (Dr Morley Read), 15b (Dr Morley Read), 16 (Wang LiQiang), 17t (Karel Bartik), 18 (Burmistrova Anastasia), 19t (scubadesign), 20–21 all (Neil Bromhall), 24 (Beverly Speed), 25t (JoramZ), 25b (Timothy Baxter), 29t (bearacreative); Wikimedia: 22 (Ingo Rechenberg), 23t (Ingo Rechenberg).

Library and Archives Canada Cataloguing in Publication

Title: Animal oddballs / Natalie Hyde.
Names: Hyde, Natalie, 1963- author.
Description: Series statement: Astonishing animals | Includes bibliographical references and index.
Identifiers: Canadiana (print) 20200155148 | Canadiana (ebook) 20200155156 | ISBN 9780778769316 (hardcover) | ISBN 9780778769378 (softcover) | ISBN 9781427124371 (HTML)
Subjects: LCSH: Animals—Juvenile literature. | LCSH Animals—Miscellanea—Juvenile literature.
Classification: LCC QL49 .H93 2020 | DDC j591—dc23

Library of Congress Cataloging-in-Publication Data

Names: Hyde, Natalie, 1963- author.
Title: Animal oddballs / Natalie Hyde.
Description: New York, New York : Crabtree Publishing Company, 2020. | Series: Astonishing animals | Includes bibliographical references and index.
Identifiers: LCCN 2019053191 (print) | LCCN 2019053192 (ebook) | ISBN 9780778769316 (hardcover) | ISBN 9780778769378 (paperback) | ISBN 9781427124371 (ebook)
Subjects: LCSH: Animals--Miscellanea--Juvenile literature. | Animal behavior--Juvenile literature.
Classification: LCC QL49 .H994 2020 (print) | LCC QL49 (ebook) | DDC 590.2--dc23
LC record available at https://lccn.loc.gov/2019053191
LC ebook record available at https://lccn.loc.gov/2019053192

Crabtree Publishing Company
www.crabtreebooks.com   1-800-387-7650

Printed in the U.S.A./022020/CG20200102

Copyright © **2020 CRABTREE PUBLISHING COMPANY.** All rights reserved. No part of this publication may be reproduced, stored in a retrieval system or be transmitted in any form or by any means, electronic, mechanical, photocopying, recording, or otherwise, without the prior written permission of Crabtree Publishing Company. In Canada: We acknowledge the financial support of the Government of Canada through the Canada Book Fund for our publishing activities.

Published in Canada
Crabtree Publishing
616 Welland Ave.
St. Catharines, Ontario
L2M 5V6

Published in the United States
Crabtree Publishing
PMB 59051
350 Fifth Avenue, 59th Floor
New York, New York 10118

Published in the United Kingdom
Crabtree Publishing
Maritime House
Basin Road North, Hove
BN41 1WR

Published in Australia
Crabtree Publishing
Unit 3 – 5 Currumbin Court
Capalaba
QLD 4157

Table of contents

Amazing animals	4
Platypuses	6
Red-headed rock agamas	8
Axolotls	10
Pangolins	12
Glass frogs	14
Shoebills	16
Immortal jellyfish	18
Naked mole rats	20
Flic-flac spiders	22
Mantis shrimp	24
North American water shrews	26
Red-lipped batfish	28
Glossary	30
Find out more	31
Index	32

Amazing animals

Creatures that live forever? Animals that can regrow their brains? Others that punch so fast they create a **shockwave**? This isn't science fiction. These animals really live among us!

Bizarre creatures

Our world is full of weird and wonderful animals. Some have **adapted** to their physical habitat, while others have developed unusual ways to protect themselves. The oddball animals in this book are each unique in their own way. They might look bizarre or have amazing abilities, but they are a perfect fit for their environment!

The star-nosed mole can "smell" underwater. It uses its uniquely shaped nose to blow air bubbles and suck them back in again.

The blue sea slug has an air bubble in its stomach, which keeps it floating near the surface of the ocean. There, its unusual blue-gray coloring keeps it hidden from **predators** above and below!

Where are they?

Every year, humans explore new places on Earth—such as deep in the jungle, under the Arctic ice, and miles down at the bottom of the ocean. Every time we explore new environments, there's a chance of discovering unusual animals. The more **remote** or difficult the landscape, the more likely it is that animals will have developed special features or behavior that help them survive there.

Platypuses

A Frankenstein creature

What animal looked so strange that the first scientists to see it thought it was a hoax? The platypus! This unusual animal has the bill of a duck, the tail of a beaver, and the body of an otter.

Egg-laying mammal

Most **mammals** give birth to live young—but not the peculiar platypus! Instead, a female platypus lays one or two eggs in her burrow in the bank of a river or pond. She holds them between her tail and body to keep them warm. The eggs hatch about ten days later. The babies are only about 1 inch (2.5 cm) long! The mother nurses them for three to four months until they can swim on their own.

Platypuses use their cheek pouches to carry their meals to the surface to eat.

Platypuses feed on water worms, shrimp, and crayfish that they find in the riverbed.

Platypuses swim with their front feet and steer with their tails.

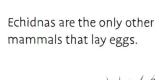

Echidnas are the only other mammals that lay eggs.

Don't mess with us!

Male platypuses have sharp spurs on their hind legs. These special stingers contain **venom** that is powerful enough to cause most creatures a lot of pain. It can even kill some small animals. During **breeding season**, males can be quick to anger. They may strike out with these spurs if they feel trapped or in danger.

FACT FILE

Found in: Eastern Australia and Tasmania

Habitat: Streams and rivers with muddy banks

Length: 20 inches (51 cm)

Diet: Worms, insects, shrimp

The platypus's dense, thick fur helps it stay warm underwater.

The platypus's webbed feet make it an excellent swimmer, so it can easily hunt for food underwater.

On land, the webbing on a platypus's feet **retracts** a bit. This reveals nails that help the animal grip the ground.

spur

Wow!

When underwater, flaps of skin cover the platypus's eyes, ears, and nostrils. But this amazing animal can still detect **prey** thanks to its super-sensitive bill.

Red-headed rock agamas

The Spider-Man lizard

Is this lizard a superhero in disguise? Its colorful scales certainly make it look like one! With its ability to climb up walls and fight off enemies, this agama lizard is definitely the master of its territory.

The color of power

The superhero colors are only found on the **dominant** male in a group of agama lizards. Just as Spider-Man puts on his brightly colored suit to fight crime, the male agama lizard's colors become brighter when he is fighting or mating. Females and lower-status males are usually an olive-brown color. When a male has secured his place as leader, he keeps his cool coloring until the next fight.

The dominant male gets first choice of spots to **bask** in the Sun.

An agama's territory is usually marked by a large rock or tree.

To become a dominant male, a lizard must find a place with no other males and establish his own group. Or he must fight another dominant male and take over his area.

Bobble-heads

Agama lizards communicate by bobbing their heads. It sometimes looks like they are doing push-ups! This nodding behavior can be a warning to another male that they are ready to fight. The dominant male will also bob his head to attract a female. Only the dominant male in a group breeds with the females.

FACT FILE

Found in: Africa, south of the Sahara Desert

Habitat: Dry, rocky terrain

Length: 5–12 inches (13–31 cm)

Diet: Insects such as ants, grasshoppers, beetles, termites

Agama lizards sit and wait for their prey to come near, then catch them with their sticky tongues.

Many comic-book fans like to keep these lizards as pets because of their superhero appearance!

Wow!

The temperature around agama eggs before they hatch determines whether they will be male or female. Lower temperatures of 78–83°F (26–28°C) produce females. Over 84°F (29°C) produces males.

Axolotls

Need a new leg? Arm? Brain? Imagine being able to regrow any part of your body so it was as good as new! That is what the axolotl, or Mexican walking fish, can do.

Brand new body parts

Axolotls can breathe through their skin as well as through their **gills**.

Although they have small teeth, axolotls usually swallow their food whole.

Wow!

Axolotls are able to regrow an arm or leg more than 100 times in a lifetime, leaving no trace of any injury!

Break a leg

Axolotls (pronounced ak-suh-lah-tuls) can grow new body parts easily. Legs, arms, eyes, even brains...if they lose one, it just grows back! **Cells** in the axolotl's body know how much of the limb is missing and can replace just as much as it needs. Scientists are closely studying axolotls to try and understand this amazing ability.

FACT FILE

Found in: Two lakes in the Valley of Mexico

Habitat: High-altitude lakes

Length: 6–18 inches (15–46 cm)

Diet: Worms, insects, small fish

Axolotls use special sensors on the sides of their heads, as well as their sense of smell, to find prey underwater.

Females lay eggs on plants near or in the water. They can lay up to 1,100 eggs in one **spawning**!

Hiding underwater

The axolotl spends almost its whole life underwater. It has gills that allow it to breathe in oxygen from the water. Wild axolotls are usually gray-brown with spots. Axolotls bred as pets are often golden colored or pinkish-white. They can change color a little to blend in with their environment and hide from predators such as storks and herons.

Pangolins

Built-in body armor

How would you like to grow your own suit of armor? That's what the pangolin does! This unusual animal protects itself with a layer of tough scales.

Suit of armor

The pangolin is the only mammal in the world that is completely covered in scales. It looks a bit like a walking pinecone! The scales are made of **keratin**, which is the same material as your fingernails. Pangolin scales are strong enough to resist bites from big beasts like lions, tigers, and leopards!

When attacked, pangolins release a terrible smell similar to skunks, from **glands** near their behind!

If a female with a baby pangolin is in danger, the little one crawls under its mother while she rolls herself into a protective ball.

Some people believe that the scales have healing properties, so pangolins are hunted for their armor.

Scaly tails

Because the scales on the pangolin overlap, no parts of its body are exposed when it moves or rolls into a ball. So, that's exactly what the animal does when it feels threatened. Even their tails have scales! This sharp tail armor is used to defend against predators such as big cats or hyenas. Pangolins can also use their tails to grab onto branches so they can hang upside down while digging for ants under the bark of trees.

FACT FILE

Found in: Central and southern Africa

Habitat: Forests and grasslands

Length: 12–39 inches (31–99 cm)

Diet: Insects, such as ants and termites

The scales make up about 20 percent of the pangolin's total bodyweight.

Pangolin scales are sharp enough to give an attacker a nasty cut.

Wow!

Pangolin scales pop out any dents by themselves. Experts are studying these scales to figure out how to create body armor that can pop out dents after being hit, so it can be reused again and again.

Glass frogs

See-through skin

Have you ever wanted to see inside a creature without hurting it? Well, now you can! Glass frogs have a **transparent** belly. You can see the frog's heart beating and lungs expanding through its skin!

Now you see them...

Glass frogs may have evolved this way as a form of camouflage. When a light shines above them, their outline on a leaf is not as prominent as other frogs'. This makes it more difficult for predators below to see them. But it's not all good news! Because their see-through skin is so thin, glass frogs absorb, or take in, **toxins** in the air or water. This often kills the frogs.

Glass frogs lay their eggs on leaves. This is safer than laying them in water, as there are more predators in water.

Male glass frogs guard the eggs. They make squeaking noises to warn other frogs to stay away.

...Now you don't

While their undersides are see-through, glass frogs' backs are spotted. The spots help the frogs blend in with their **clutch** of eggs. This helps disguise the males that are protecting them! Sometimes, males kick their back legs at wasps that buzz around, trying to eat the eggs.

FACT FILE

Found in: Mexico, Central and South America

Habitat: Treetops of rain forests

Length: 0.75–1.5 inches (1.9–3.8 cm)

Diet: Spiders and insects

vein

heart

intestines

Wow!
Through the transparent abdomen, you can see the large vein that carries blood through the frog's body!

15

Shoebills

A huge, silent killer

Do you think a bird that grows taller than you is only found in nightmares and horror movies? Think again! The prehistoric-looking African shoebill stork can grow up to 5 feet (1.5 m) tall.

Bird statue

A bird as big as the shoebill cannot sneak up on its prey very well, so it has a different **strategy**. It stands perfectly still—and waits for prey to come to it! Shoebills are known to stay silent for days. These birds are so big that they are not even afraid to hunt and eat young crocodiles.

Shoebills can be aggressive if people get too close. They will lunge forward with their big beak open.

There are thought to be between 5,000 and 8,000 shoebills living in the wild.

Shoebills mostly stay quiet, but they can make quite a racket when they want to. When a shoebill sees another bird, it greets it by clattering its bill together loudly!

A shoebill's beak is a deadly weapon. When it sees prey, such as eels or lungfish, it plunges its razor-sharp bill into the mud to scoop it up whole.

FACT FILE

Found in: East Africa

Habitat: Freshwater swamps

Height: 43–55 inches (109–140 cm)

Diet: Large fish, snakes, lizards

Rarely seen birds

The shoebill's ability to hide silently in the tall grasses of African swamplands meant modern scientists didn't discover them until 1850! Today, humans are the shoebill's biggest predator. Because they are so rare and mysterious, they are a target for **poachers** who hunt them to sell to private collectors. The birds are now at risk of **extinction**.

Wow!
These big birds can live up to 35 years—that's a long lifespan for a bird!

After scooping up its prey, the shoebill swings its head from side to side to get rid of mud and plants before gulping down its victim.

Immortal jellyfish

How would you like to go back to your childhood and start over again? The immortal jellyfish can do just that. As its name suggests, this weird sea creature never dies!

Restarts its life over and over and over...

body

mouth

tentacle

During the "medusa" phase of its life (see page 19), the jellyfish's body is shaped like an umbrella.

Like other jellyfish, the immortal jellyfish has no brain or heart.

18

Tiny jellyfish

An immortal jellyfish starts life like all other jellyfish: as **larva** called planula. The planula attach themselves to the sea floor and create a colony of **polyps**. There, they develop into medusas—free-moving jellyfish. Even when fully grown, these jellyfish are tiny—only about as wide as your pinky finger.

FACT FILE

Found in: Oceans around the world

Habitat: Warmer waters

Width: 0.15–0.2 inches (4–5 mm)

Diet: Plankton, larvae, and fish eggs

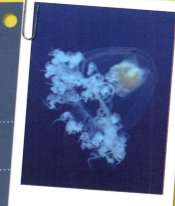

The tube-like jellyfish polyp has a mouth at the top surrounded by tentacles for catching food.

When the jellyfish restarts its life, its body creates new cells and tissue, so it's really a whole new creature!

Wow!

Immortal jellyfish can have young with or without a **mate**. In the right conditions, they can release eggs once a day!

Starting over

The immortal jellyfish never grows old. Once it has had its young, it reverts to a polyp. Its tentacles retract, its body shrinks, and it sinks to the sea floor. Then it starts over. Immortal jellyfish only die if they are eaten by a predator, such as a sea slug, or suffer from a disease.

Naked mole rats

Super-surviving rodent

Can an odd-looking rodent hold the key to beating cancer? Naked mole rats may not look pretty, but scientists are studying their amazing ability to stay healthy and survive in tough conditions.

Naked mole rats can live for up to 18 minutes underground with no oxygen at all!

Survivor

Naked mole rats have no fur or hair on their wrinkly bodies. They spend their entire lives underground, eating the roots and **tubers** of plants growing above them. They can survive in tunnels, where there is not much oxygen in the air. They rarely get cancer and live longer than most rodents their size. Scientists are trying to figure out why this is!

Naked mole rats do not get a mouthful of dirt when they dig new tunnels because their front teeth are outside their lips.

Cooperation is key

Naked mole rats are one of the few mammals that live in a social community. Young rats are cared for by a whole group. Different groups in the community have different jobs. Worker groups dig tunnels and carry dirt to the surface. Only one rat—the queen—has babies. She may have up to 30 pups in one litter, and as many as 60 pups per year!

FACT FILE

Found in: East Africa

Habitat: Dry grasslands

Length: 3–13 inches (8–33 cm)

Diet: Underground roots

> Structured communities with a queen, workers, guards, etc. are common among insects, but mole rats are the only mammals to live like this.

> Many generations of rats will live in one colony.

Wow!

Naked mole rats can move their two front teeth separately, like a pair of chopsticks!

Flic-flac spiders

Unusual escape plan

Ever heard of a spider that can do gymnastics? Well, take a trip to the desert in Morocco and you might just see one! When the flic-flac spider needs to escape predators, it does handsprings across the sand dunes.

Desert dweller

The flic-flac spider is a type of huntsman spider found in North Africa. It is **nocturnal**, spending the hours of darkness wandering over the sand, feeding on its favorite moths until the Sun comes up. Its movements are perfectly normal (for a spider). But when it spots a predator, it springs into action—literally! It can flip forward or backward to escape quickly.

The flic-flac spider can even flip uphill!

Some other huntsman spiders use a cartwheel-type movement, but only the flic-flac spider uses a handspring.

Wow!

The flic-flac spider's handsprings can reach 4.5 miles per hour (7.2 kph). At that speed, they'd beat some runners in the New York marathon!

I, robot

The flic-flac spider was discovered by a bionics professor, Ingo Rechenberg. Bionics is the process of copying animal and human movements with machines. Rechenberg was so fascinated by the spider's handsprings that he helped to design a robot that uses the same motion to move quickly across different surfaces.

FACT FILE

Found in: The Sahara Desert in Morocco

Habitat: Sand dunes

Length: 0.5–0.8 inches (1.3–2 cm)

Diet: Insects, such as moths

The company that built the robot says it will be useful for moving across tough surfaces in harsh conditions, such as on the sea floor—or even on Mars!

The robot's name, Tabbot, is based on the Berber word "tabacha," which means "spider."

Mantis shrimp

Supersonic punch

Which creature can deliver a knockout punch at the bottom of the sea? The mantis shrimp! This underwater champ is strong enough to smash through the shells of its prey!

How fast?

The mantis shrimp has a secret weapon: two hinged arms, or clubs, that it keeps folded under its head. When prey comes along or a predator attacks, these clubs come out from its body at an incredible 50 miles per hour (80 kph)! **Friction** from the motion makes the water around them boil. When the bubbles from the boiling water burst, they create a shockwave of energy in the ocean!

- The eyes of the mantis shrimp are located on stalks on the top of its head, and can move independently.

- Clubs swing out from beneath the head.

- Mantis shrimp are nicknamed "thumb splitters" because of the painful gash they can cause if people do not handle them carefully.

Power of the punch

With such a powerful punch, how does the mantis shrimp not hurt itself when it makes contact? Inside the clubs are **fibers** that act like shock absorbers. They prevent the clubs from cracking and breaking. Mantis shrimp limbs are so strong that scientists are studying them to improve body armor for soldiers!

FACT FILE

Found in: Oceans worldwide

Habitat: Burrows and rocks in the seabed

Length: 4–18 inches (10–46 cm)

Diet: Fish, crabs, worms, and other shrimp

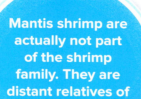

Mantis shrimp are actually not part of the shrimp family. They are distant relatives of crabs and lobsters.

The female mantis shrimp lays two clutches of eggs. She looks after one and the male takes care of the other.

Wow!

Mantis shrimp are rarely kept in aquariums. With a punch carrying a force 100 times its weight, the shrimp can crack a glass tank!

After hatching, mantis shrimps may live for up to 20 years.

North American water shrews

Water walkers

Is walking on water just an illusion? Not if you're a water shrew! Its ability to run across the surface has earned it the nickname "Jesus shrew" after the story in the Bible that describes how Jesus walked on water.

Hairy feet

The secret to the water shrew's trick is its feet, which are fringed with hair. When bubbles of air get trapped in the hair or fur on its feet, they create a sort of cushion. This allows the water shrew to scoot along the surface, like a hovercraft, for up to five seconds. That's just enough time to get away from predators such as owls or giant salamanders!

The water shrew's thick fur keeps it warm by trapping air in the layers. The coat is also water-resistant.

North American water shrews are one of the largest shrew species, but they still only weigh about the same as a AAA battery!

Sensitive snout

Water shrews eat insects and small animals from the water and on land. They do not have good eyesight, so they use their flexible **snouts** and sensitive whiskers and lips to seek out their prey. When hunting underwater, their whiskers detect **sound waves**, as well as physical waves from the slightest motion. That lets them know that lunch may be nearby!

FACT FILE

Found in: Northern USA and Canada

Habitat: Plains and mountains near water

Length: 5–6.7 inches (13–17 cm)

Diet: Water insects, land insects, fish, small mammals

In addition to walking on water, these shrews are great swimmers and divers!

North American water shrews will dip beneath the surface to feed on underwater creatures.

Wow!

These water shrews can dive as deep as 6.5 feet (2 m) and stay underwater for up to 60 seconds!

27

Red-lipped batfish

Would you like to kiss a fish? Well, the red-lipped batfish seems ready to pucker up! Its bright red lips look like they were smeared with lipstick.

A fish that doesn't like to swim!

Bat or fish?

The red-lipped batfish is a fish shaped like a bat. It can swim, but it usually doesn't. It prefers to use its fins to walk along the ocean floor. By standing on its fins, it can have a good look around for something tasty to eat!

The red-lipped batfish's spotted brown and beige back helps it blend into the ocean floor.

Researchers think the batfish's bright red lips are used to attract a mate.

Come to me!

The red-lipped batfish is a type of anglerfish. Like other anglerfish, it has a **lure** on the top of its head. This horn covered in little hairs can be pulled in or out, depending on whether or not it is dinner time. When the lure is out, small fish and **crustaceans** mistake it for something good to eat. By then it's too late—they become the batfish's next meal!

FACT FILE

Found in: Galápagos Islands and off the coast of Peru

Habitat: Ocean floor

Length: 8 inches (20 cm)

Diet: Other small fish, shrimp, mollusks

Red-lipped batfish can swim, but they are slow and awkward when they do.

These fish have no natural predators and may live for up to 12 years.

 lure

Wow!

Red-lipped batfish can be found on the edges of reefs as deep as 390 feet (119 m)—that's deeper than the length of a football field.

Glossary

adapted Changed to fit a new purpose

bask To lie in the Sun

breeding season The time of year when an animal mates and has babies

cell The smallest unit that makes up all living things

clutch A group of eggs

crustacean One of a group of sea creatures with hard outer skeletons, such as crabs, lobsters, and shrimps

dominant Describing the top or most powerful position in a group

extinction When a species of plant or animal dies out completely, so there are no more left

fiber A long, thin thread

friction The force created when one surface rubs against another

gills Organs that let sea creatures take oxygen from the water

gland An organ in the body that produces substances, such as sweat, that have specific uses in the body

keratin The strong substance that forms hair, fingernails, hoofs, and horns

larva The immature form of some animals; larvae often look like worms

lure Something that acts as bait and attracts something else

mammal An animal that is warm-blooded and usually gives birth to live young

mate An animal that another animal breeds with to have babies

nocturnal Active at night

poacher Someone who hunts animals illegally

polyp A stage in an animal's life cycle; polyps are often tube-shaped

predators Animals that hunt other animals for food

prey Animals that are hunted for food by other animals

remote Far away and hard to get to

retract Go back inside

shockwave A wave of energy that travels through air or water

snout The nose and mouth of an animal that sticks out

sound wave A type of vibration that can be heard

spawning When fish lay their eggs

strategy A plan of action

transparent See-through

toxins Poisonous substances

tuber A thick, round root, like a potato

venom Poison

Find out more

Books
Ghigna, Charles. *Strange, Unusual, Gross & Cool Animals*. Animal Planet, 2016.

Keating, Jess. *Cute as an Axolotl*. Knopf Books for Young Readers, 2018.

National Geographic Kids. *Weird But True Animals*. National Geographic Children's Books, 2018.

Websites
https://bit.ly/2L3sG95
Check out these weird and mind-blowing animal facts.

https://nationalzoo.si.edu/animals/naked-mole-rat
Find out all about naked mole rats and watch them live at the Smithsonian's National Zoo and Conservation Biology Institute.

www.natgeokids.com/uk/discover/animals/sea-life/strange-sea-creatures/
Check out the ocean's weirdest creatures at National Geographic Kids.

Index

adaptations 4
armor 12, 13, 25
axolotls 10–11

behavior 5, 8, 9
bills 6, 7, 16, 17
blood 15
blue sea slugs 5
brains 4, 10, 11, 18
breathing 10, 11

cancer 20
clubs 24, 25
coloring 5, 8, 9, 11

echidnas 7
eggs 6, 9, 14, 15, 19, 25
extinction 17
eyes 7, 11, 24

feet 6, 7, 26
fighting 8, 9
fins 28

flic-flac spiders 22–23
food 6, 7, 9, 10, 11, 13, 15, 16, 17, 19, 21, 23, 25, 27, 29
fur 7, 20, 26

gills 10, 11
glass frogs 14–15

hearts 14, 15, 18

immortal jellyfish 18–19

lungs 14
lures 29

mammals 6, 12, 21
mantis shrimp 24–25
mating 7, 8, 19, 29

naked mole rats 20–21
North American water shrews 26–27

oxygen 11, 20

pangolins 12–13
pets 9, 11
platypuses 6–7
poachers 17
predators 5, 11, 13, 14, 17, 19, 24, 29

Rechenberg, Ingo 23
red-headed rock agamas 8–9

scales 12, 13
shoebills 16–17
star-nosed moles 4

tails 6, 13
teeth 20, 21
tentacles 18, 19
toxins 14
tunnels 20, 21

venom 7